The Little Lambs

Rainy Day

Illustrations by José-Luis Macias S.
Original story by M.C. Suigne
Retold by Linda L. Booth

Maggie has a lot of work to do today. Her dog, Brownie, helps her as much as he can.

While Maggie is milking the cow, her neighbor and friend, Matthew, comes to find her. "Everyone's going to visit Maria — please come too."

Maggie and Matthew gather the little lambs into a flock so they can take them with them to their friend's house in the mountains.

"Let's have a picnic lunch in the meadow," suggests Maggie.

The thirsty little lambs refresh themselves after the journey.
Brownie wants to play with Nony, the little black lamb.

But ploof! Nony falls into the water! Brownie barks excitedly till the children come to her rescue.

"Nony, please stay with the other lambs—we're ready for our picnic now," Maria says sweetly.

Oh no! Just as they finish setting out the picnic, big raindrops begin to fall.

"Quick, get the lambs," cries Maggie. But Nony, forever curious, is looking around. . . .

A big crack of lightning frightens little Nony right off the mountain's edge! Our small friends hurry the animals to shelter. . . .

. . .then rescue little Nony who has had the good luck to land on a tree, and hang on. The children have thought clearly and acted bravely, even though it's windy and rainy.

Matthew carefully lights a fire. After their clothes dry, they'll
finally have their lovely picnic. . .indoors. . .with Nony right by
their side!

Published in the United States and simultaneously in Canada by Joshua Morris, In
431 Post Road East, Westport, CT 068
Printed in Belgiu